ACE VENTURA
PET DETECTIVE

TM

The Case
of the
Hollywood
Hound

By Jesse Leon McCann

SCHOLASTIC INC.

New York   Toronto   London   Auckland   Sydney
Mexico City   New Delhi   Hong Kong

For James Nash, who loves a mystery.
Thanks for helping when I needed it most.

No part of this publication may be reproduced in whole or in part, or stored in a retrieval system, or transmitted in any form or by any means, electronic, mechanical, photocopying, recording, or otherwise, without written permission of the publisher. For information regarding permission, write to Scholastic Inc., Attention: Permissions Department, 555 Broadway, New York, NY 10012.

ISBN 0-439-20862-9

Copyright © 2001 by Morgan Creek Productions, Inc.
All rights reserved.
Published by Scholastic Inc.
SCHOLASTIC and associated logos are trademarks and/or registered trademarks of Scholastic Inc.
Designed by Keirsten Geise

12 11 10 9 8 7 6 5 4 3 2 1   1 2 3 4 5 6/0

Printed in the U.S.A.

First Scholastic printing, March 2001

Ace's Theme Song

Ace Ventura, Pet Detective
Alrighty then!
He can sniff like a dog
He's slippery as a frog
Ace Ventura!
Radar like a bat
He's a way cool cat
That's Ace
If there's a tail
He's on the trail
He's sooo protective!
Even if his brain seems defective
Ace Ventura, Pet Detective
He can roar back in time
'N' save a dino in distress
Ace Ventura
He'll squash an alien bug
Eeeeuuuuw . . .
What a mess!
Ooooo, Ace!
He's pesky as a flea
Stings like a bee
Swings like a monkey and . . .
. . . Oooo what a hunk . . .
He's Ace Ventura, Pet Detective
Ace Ventura!
Alrighty then!

"The city . . . Miami, Florida. It was a cold and rainy night. I was sitting at my desk, listening to the raindrops rapping briskly against the window of my office. I'm Ace Ventura, Pet Detective, and I carry a badge — Animal Planet member #436, that's me, sweetheart.

"Suddenly, I realized it wasn't the rain beating against the chilly glass that I was hearing! It was my semi-faithful simian sidekick, Spike the wonder monkey, cracking walnuts on his lumpy forehead!"

Spike stopped mid-crack, his knuckles pressing a walnut against his brow. He frowned. Every time Ace had gotten bored lately, he'd start pretending he was a movie detective narrating his own mystery story. What a nut! And speaking of nuts . . .

"Ah, ha!" Ace yelled, as he leaped to his feet. He pointed an accusing finger at

Spike. "So, Professor Monkey! I've caught you red-handed with the Maltese Walnuts — and I believe you *weren't* going to share!"

The little monkey rolled his eyes. He hoped they got a new case soon, before Ace went totally stir-crazy.

"And so ends another adventure from the tattered casebook of Ace Ventura, Pet Detective! All-righty-then!"

Ace crossed the dimly lit room and looked out the glass of his office door. "But never fear, devoted fans! A new adventure is sure to begin soon. For whenever a pet is in trouble, Ace Ventura is there! When the call of the wild comes, I'll be ready!"

Ace put his nose to the window and peered out into the darkness. A moment later, he realized a twitchy face was outside staring right back at him.

"*Yahhhhhh!*" Ace jumped back and screamed suddenly, causing Spike to throw the walnuts he was eating into the air. "A

2

giant, monstrous, genetically enhanced rodent! And it's not Mickey Mouse!"

There was a loud tapping on the door. A man poked his head in. He had a thin, long face, and Spike thought he *did* resemble a rat, in a creepy sort of way.

"Pardon me. . . . I didn't mean to frighten you," the man said.

"Frighten me? Nonsense! I scoff at danger! *Scoff! Scoff!*" Ace waved in the man's direction. "I merely thought you were a science experiment gone horribly awry. It would take a lot more than *that* to frighten me!"

"My name is Frankie Fester," the man said with a nervous laugh. "I'm a Hollywood talent agent."

"*Eeeeeeek!* A Hollywood agent?!" Ace jumped up on his desk, pulled his pant legs up in terror, and hopped around nervously. "Get him away! Get him away!!"

"Please, Mr. Ventura, I need your help!" Frankie pleaded. "Have you ever heard of 'Sparky the famous Hollywood star'?"

Ace calmed himself and sat down coolly on the edge of his desk. He nonchalantly examined his fingernails.

"Do you mean the movie star canine? The star of such mega-blockbuster hits as *Sparky Versus the Venusian Dog Catcher*?" he asked casually.

"Yes!"

"*Sparky Joins the Navy Seals*?" Ace asked.

"The very same!" Frankie Fester replied eagerly.

"Sorry. Never heard of him," Ace yawned.

Frankie pulled an envelope out of his pocket. "Sparky's been kidnapped, Mr. Ventura! The police are baffled and I need your help. These are plane tickets for you and Spike. Meet me in Hollywood tomorrow."

Spike was sure it was the mention of a missing pet that convinced Ace to say yes.

But a chance to visit Hollywood made the decision easy. They had a new case!

The ratlike little man said his good-byes and left. Then Ace and Spike began packing all the things they'd need for this important detective work: swim trunks, tanning oil, a beach ball . . .

"Gravy, Spike, my often-honest hairy cohort!" Ace grinned happily. "Once more the pet detective business leads us to an exotic locale! The *bright lights* of a California movie studio — about as different from *this* place as you can possibly get!"

Just then, *krack-a-thoom!* — a big bolt of lightning flashed outside, and the office was plunged into total darkness. The power was out. And Ace and Spike heard the sound of the office door opening and closing.

"See what I mean?"

It didn't take long for the power to be restored. But when it was, Ace and Spike got a big surprise. There was something tacked to Ace's office door that hadn't been there before.

It was a dog collar. The name "Sparky" was on the tag. And there was a note that read:

STAY OFF THE CASE . . . OR ELSE!

"Like most pet gumshoes, I don't like to be threatened. Nothing would keep me from saving an animal in trouble. My main monkey, Spike, and I caught the first plane to Los Angeles.

"The city was wrapped in a predawn mist as the pilot turned on the fasten seat belts sign to prepare for landing. As usual, my mind was busy trying to unlock the answer to an important mystery — one that's bothered a lot of Joes for a *long* time.

"Hey! How come these honey-roasted nuts don't come in bigger packets?" Ace waved to a passing flight attendant. "If they were bigger, we wouldn't have to keep asking for more!"

"Oob ookla hoob!" Spike scowled at Ace with a furrowed brow, briefly plucking off his earphones. *I'm trying to watch the in-flight movie here!*

8

"Sorry, Spike. You know how restless I get on airplanes," Ace explained sheepishly. "Wanna play 'there's some*thing* on the wing' again?" Ace jammed his face up against his window and squealed, "It's out there, I tell ya! It looked right at me!"

Spike didn't want to play.

Luckily for everyone, the plane landed smoothly just a few minutes later. A limousine was waiting for Ace and Spike. They were quickly whisked away from the airport and were at the Dream Factory movie studio in no time.

Frankie Fester met them at a soundstage where Sparky's latest movie, *Sparky Saves the Farm*, was being filmed.

"Sparky was rehearsing right over there," Frankie pointed to a set that looked like the inside of an old log cabin. "They were just about to shoot a scene, when the lights suddenly blew out. When they came back on a few minutes later, Sparky was gone!"

"Re-hee-hee-heally?" Ace asked slyly. "That sounds *very* familiar, doesn't it, Spike?"

"Hoo bloob ook ook!" Spike nodded in a distracted way. His mind was busy with a more important puzzle. Namely, where was the catering truck? He went off to investigate.

"Sounds to me like a spoiled animal actor that won't keep up with the filming schedule!" said a prim figure walking their way.

"Oh, no!" whispered Frankie, pointing to the woman in sharp business clothes who was approaching them. "It's Ms. Astor, the head of the movie studio. I'm sure she's not very happy about all this. It's costing the studio a fortune each day the film is delayed."

Indeed, Ms. Astor did not seem very happy. As she drew near, she gave Ace a frown.

"I suppose you're that absurd pet detective person," Ms. Astor said sourly.

"And I suppose," answered Ace, "you've been sucking on lemons."

"I *beg* your pardon?!"

"I said, glad you could drop in." Ace smiled smoothly. "How's that wicked sister of yours from the East? Any houses fall on her lately?"

Ms. Astor turned away from Ace to Frankie Fester.

"Listen, Fester. If that dog can't be found soon, your so-called superstar will be replaced by another animal," she said.

"Just give us a little more time, Ms. Astor!" Frankie pleaded. "The police couldn't find any clues. That's why I called in Mr. Ventura. If anyone can find Sparky, he can!"

Frankie looked very worried. "B-Besides, that dog is a national treasure! Did you know there was a big reward posted for Sparky's return? All of Hollywood is donating to the cause."

"I'll give you exactly one day," Ms. Astor turned away curtly. "In the meantime, I've ordered the film's director to start a casting call for Sparky's replacement. I want to be prepared."

Ms. Astor gave a dismissive wave of the hand, then walked over to talk to some stagehands, leaving Ace and Frankie alone.

"Wel-l-l-l-l! Who put the extra starch in her shorts?" Ace asked. "She doesn't care much for Sparky, does she?"

"She's just jealous," Frankie replied. "Sparky gets all the attention. He deserves a big raise. He can't help it if he's a big star."

"Yes, it's a dog-eat-dog world," Ace remarked. "When will people realize that animals are people, too? If we just let them be, they'll stay out of trouble."

Just then, Ace and Frankie heard a

shout from the other end of the sound-stage.

"Get him! Grab that monkey!"

Ace sighed. "We-hee-ll, *most* animals stay out of trouble!"

Chapter 3

Ace rushed to the other side of the sound-stage to rescue Spike. When Ace arrived, he saw a tall man holding Spike in the air.

"All right, drop the monkey and step away!"

"Ood goop chee chee oot!" Spike waved Ace back. *Go away! Can't you see I'm auditioning?*

"Auditioning?" Ace gulped.

The tall man put Spike down on the floor, turned to Ace and smiled. "Ah, you must be the monkey's manager! He's absolutely brilliant! Why he could be a star in Hollywood . . . no, more than a star . . . a screen legend!"

The man used his hands to make a frame and peered at Spike through it. The little monkey was tap-dancing across the floor.

The man put his arm around Ace's shoulders and took him aside. He pulled out a roll of paper. The paper unrolled and hit the floor. Ace saw that it was a contract.

"I'm 'Hank' Henderson, the world-renowned film director," the man gushed. "If you sign this short agreement, your little monkey could be the next great animal star! Think of the list he'll join: Lassie, Francis the talking mule, Benji, Free Willy, Stallone, Sparky . . . and Spike!"

"Gee-hee-hee, let me think . . . no." Ace plucked Hank Henderson's hand from his shoulder, picked up Spike, and carried the disappointed monkey away. "My sometimes-efficient fuzzy partner would never leave me for a life of movie monkey starlets! Ta-ta now. Buh-bye!"

Ace started crossing the soundstage. "What a looooooser! Imagine thinking you'd trade an exciting career of pet detecting for a glamorous life in the movies — constantly surrounded by adoring fans, riding in limos, and going to fancy parties!" Suddenly, Ace realized Spike wasn't listening. In fact, he wasn't with Ace! The little monkey was back with Hank Henderson, reading the contract with pen in hand.

"Spike!" Ace cried. He ran over and snatched the monkey, then hauled him back across the set.

Back at the farmhouse set, they heard the sound of excited talking. Frankie was really upset and he was begging Ms. Astor for something. Standing with them was a snooty-looking man holding a large, chubby dog with lots of wrinkles.

"Please, Ms. Astor! Don't think about using any other dogs . . . until Mr. Ventura gets a chance to look for Sparky!" Frankie cried.

Ms. Astor was not moved. "Nonsense! Sparky isn't the only dog star in Hollywood, and you aren't the only agent!"

Ms. Astor pointed to the snooty man with the dog. "This is my brother, Philip," Ms. Astor said. "He is also an agent and he has brought his client, Duke, to audition for Sparky's part."

"Aw, no . . . no!" cried Frankie.

Hank Henderson walked up just then. "Okay, people! Let's see what this new dog can do . . . although I have my doubts now. Now, if only we could replace Sparky with a monkey. . . ."

Spike grinned winningly.

"Don't even think about it!" Ace frowned.

Henderson sighed and sat down in his director's chair. "Very well. Let's see the new dog. Ready? Action!"

Philip Astor sat Duke down. The chunky dog immediately picked up a prop sword and skull and held them high in the air. Frankie couldn't watch. He ran from the set with his hands over his face.

"Rorfh rrrww hhrrr? Bowww wowww!" Duke began to emote pompously. *To be, or not to be? That is the question!*

Hmmph! I could do that! Spike

thought. He sniffed as he sat down in the chair next to Henderson.

Henderson was watching carefully. "Hmm. Duke does have *some* talent. Perhaps with a little work . . ."

Spike was incredulous. *What?! He's not going to hire that dog, is he? Duke's a big buffoon!* Spike thought he might just go on the set, knock Duke out of the way, and show them what real acting was all about!

Then, suddenly, the lights went out. The soundstage was plunged into complete darkness!

"You know, that's been happening a lot lately!" Ace observed.

The lights came back on a few moments later. But the dog was gone! Duke had vanished! Everyone gasped.

Then again, Spike thought, *if Duke wants the part, he can have it.*

Chapter 4

"The faces of everyone in the room were as white as ghosts. I immediately jumped up to where Duke had been standing and began to snoop around. It didn't take long to see that whoever was stealing these dogs was a real pro . . . and he could lift a lot of weight, 'cause Duke was no taco-eating chihuahua!

"No visible tracks. No prints. No clues at all! At least, so it would seem to the untrained eye. But Ace Ventura, Pet Detective is on the case!"

"Who is he talking to?" Ms. Astor asked sharply.

"He's a little strange, but I hear he's the best," Frankie said apologetically.

Philip Astor was livid. "This is outrageous! I demand that Duke be returned at once!"

"Calm down, Philip dear," Ms. Astor commanded her brother. "I'm going to hire a real detective instead of this buffoon."

"Why hire the rest when you've already got the best? Ace Ventura will solve this little disappearing act!" Ace declared. "Now stand aside as my itchy half-pint primate pal Spike and I go to work. . . . Spike? Spike?"

Ace and the others looked around. Spike wasn't standing with them any longer. A short search revealed that he had wandered over to the makeup table and was having his nails done by a manicurist.

"Spike!" Ace asked crossly, "What in the name of Scooby-Doo do you think you're doing??"

"Oob a-coop ook eep eep?" Spike replied. *I have to look nice for my fans, don't I?*

Ace grabbed Spike and carried him back to the farmhouse set. "Honestly, Spike. I never thought you'd be one to get stagestruck!"

Spike just shrugged.

"Alrighty then, Spike!" Ace smiled as he put the little monkey down. "I need your powerful, food-finding nose to help me. I'm picking up the faint scent of a clue. Smell that?"

Spike *could* smell something. He started sniffing and walking around the set with his nose close to the floor, like a bloodhound. Ace, also sniffing and bent over, followed right behind him.

"This is ridiculous!" Philip Astor stamped his foot like a spoiled little kid. "Duke is missing and these two clowns are just wasting time!"

"I beg to differ, poopy-pants!" Ace said with a grin. "For you see, my hairy little Watson and I have found your hefty hound!"

Ace bent down and pulled at one of the floorboards. To everyone's surprise, Ace lifted up a trapdoor. They all ran up and peered inside. There, surrounded by dozens of dog biscuits, was Duke, scared out of his wits.

"You see, when the lights went out, someone opened the trapdoor and pushed Duke inside," Ace explained. "The trail of dog biscuits leads off under the soundstage. Whoever did this was hoping Duke would follow the trail of yummy-looking biscuits."

"But Duke wouldn't eat those!" Philip Astor exclaimed as he gathered up his shivering client. "He only eats gourmet dog biscuits."

"You are correct, sir! And that's where the dognapper made a big mistake," Ace declared jumping through the trapdoor. "C'mon, Spike! If we follow these biscuits, they'll lead us right to the culprit!"

Spike didn't need to be asked twice. He eagerly jumped under the soundstage. Those dog biscuits looked delicious — gourmet or not!

"But what about my poor Duke?"

Philip Astor cried, holding out the dog. "He can't act in this condition!"

"Oh, boo-hoo! Why don't you cry me a river, build a bridge, and get over it?" Ace suggested. "Ta-ta. Buh-bye now!"

Ace and Spike followed the trail of dog biscuits underneath the soundstage. The path wound around support pillars and through a door that led outside.

Now they were out on the studio lot, passing people working on different kinds of movies. There were actors and stagehands, prop people and technicians. Spike really felt in his element as he followed behind Ace, munching happily on dog biscuits.

Maybe I should *quit working for Ace and become a movie star,* Spike pondered.

"Eureka . . . and I'm not talkin' about the vacuum cleaner!" Ace smiled and pointed ahead to a big warehouse. "Spike, my arm-dragging *amigo,* the clues lead to the prop department! Little does the thief know that we are right on his trail. Come on!"

Ace and Spike sneaked toward the property warehouse, following the dog biscuits.

Little did they know that a mysterious stranger in the shadows was right on *their* trail.

Chapter 5

"The prop warehouse was dark and eerie. Years of dust and spiderwebs covered the place in a creepy way, like if Mandy Moore covered a No Doubt song."

"Stuff from old movie productions rose up around us like piles of stinky socks the night before wash day. There were pirate props, things from monster movies, and junk from science-fiction epics.

"Most of the stuff looked so *real* — like that Tiki-god statue that seemed to be looking at me . . . it *was* looking at me! It was moving toward me with its arms outstretched! It growled!"

"Hrrrrowwwwl!"

"*Aaaaaagh!* Don't put the ancient evil eye on me! I'll be good, really I will! I'll even eat my peas!"

Just then, Ace heard a quiet chuckling. Monkey chuckling. He frowned at the Tiki statue.

"Spike, is that you?"

Now Spike was full-out laughing. While Ace had been wandering around pretending to be a movie detective, the little monkey had crawled into the Tiki prop. He thought he might be able to scare Ace, and he was right! He really was a great actor!

"I knew it was you all along," Ace fibbed. "I was merely . . . testing you."

Spike wasn't buying it. He just giggled.

Ace glowered. "Now, if you're through fooling around, we can get back to work!"

Ace turned to examine a huge pile of sci-fi props. He poked his head into the pile to get a better look. Then he jumped back and screamed! There was a horrible-looking alien creature attached to his face!

"Help! It's a face-hugger!" Ace bellowed. "I'm doomed! Doomed!"

Spike was in a panic. He didn't know

what to do. Ace was rolling around on the floor now, crying out in agony!

The little monkey took a deep breath, leaped on top of Ace and began pulling at the slimy alien thing with all his might! He tugged . . . and tugged . . . and finally the creature came off and went soaring back into the pile.

Spike didn't want to look! What had the thing done to Ace's poor face? He must be horribly disfigured. Finally, Spike took a peek.

Ace was smiling a big smile. "Gotcha!"

They both laughed and laughed. No matter how serious the case, the two friends always managed to have fun. Ace continued chuckling as he put the Tiki statue back in its spot. Spike happily munched on the dog biscuits he'd found.

"Alrighty then! Enough tomfoolery! There's an animal in danger. Time to get back on the trail of our puppy-napper!"

But when Ace went to look for the dog

biscuit trail, it was gone. Spike had eaten all the biscuits in the area! Ace couldn't tell which way to go. Ace frowned at Spike. Spike grinned guiltily.

"Spike! I can't believe you ate our clues! That's not proper behavior for an experienced pet detective assistant!"

Now Spike was in a huff. *"Chee chee oop a-la chee! Ooka ooka chee eep,"* the little monkey said haughtily. *Maybe I don't want to be your assistant anymore. Maybe I want to be a movie star!*

Ace was stunned. "What are you saying, Spike?"

They both fell quiet. Neither was sure what to say. And in that quiet moment, they heard it . . .

"Creeeeak!"

Startled, they peered though the dusty warehouse in the direction of the sound. An inky-black figure moved in the shadows.

"Don't look now, Spike, but I think

we've got company," Ace whispered. "We've got to get out of here. It could be the dognapper trying to trap us!"

They sneaked away, around old desk chairs, lamps, cabinets, and piles of carpeting. But whoever was following them stayed close behind.

So Ace and Spike went faster and faster, around model battleships and in between fake rock piles. Still the mysterious stranger stayed on their heels. They couldn't lose him!

Now Ace and Spike were running as fast as they could, past Native American tepees, through a miniature city, and over a giant pencil. They fled past rows and rows of antique guns, Civil War swords, and Viking shields. They turned a corner — it was a dead end.

They could hear the stranger's footsteps getting closer. Then, the footsteps stopped. Ace and Spike looked at each other.

"Maybe he doesn't want to play any-more, and went home," Ace said hopefully.

Spike smirked at him. *Yeah, right!*

Suddenly, a shelf next to them began to shake and rattle. Things started to fall from it. Ace and Spike looked up, and what they saw horrified them.

Dozens of Zulu warrior spears were falling toward them, points-first!

Chapter 6

Fortunately, Ace had had spears thrown at him before — he knew just what to do! He quickly grabbed Spike and began to dodge the rain of spears, darting this way and that.

"Jump to the left, turn to the right, do the hokey-pokey, and fight, fight, fight!" Ace pranced through the falling spears like a lord of the dance. "Good thing I bought those cheerleading practice tapes, eh, Spike?"

Spike was impressed.

The last spear was falling past them now. It barely missed them, just grazing Ace's head. But it was just enough to mess up his hair a little.

"That does it!" Ace was fuming now, pointing at his hair. "Nobody messes with the 'do!"

Ace sprinted down the hall, with Spike close behind him. In the shadows they could see the mysterious stranger slinking away.

"As a duly appointed pet detective, I order you to halt!"

But the figure just kept walking. Ace grabbed a lasso from an Old West shelf. "I'm sorry, but you leave me no choice!" He roped the intruder like a cowboy at a rodeo. *"Eee-yaah!"*

The lasso wrapped quickly around the figure. Soon the intruder was lying on the floor, trussed up like a Christmas ham.

"Now, let's see who we've got here," Ace said as he dragged the man out of the shadows.

They'd never seen him before. He was short and squat, with big bags under his eyes. Ace decided to question him. They put the man in a chair and turned on some lamps they found in the corner. The man squinted in the bright light.

Then Ace began the interrogation . . .

by bending over and moving his butt-cheeks.

"I'm Special Agent *Flanksteak* from the FBI — the Federal *Buttocks* Investigators — and I mean to get to the *bottom* of this! Who are you? What are you doing here?"

The man began to sweat. "My name is Sam Shovel and I'm a security detective, working for the studio!"

"Yeah, well, that doesn't explain why you were bringing up the *rear,* or why you inter*rump*ted our investigation," Ace countered.

"I-I was just trying to see if I could help find Sparky. If I did, it would mean a huge bonus for me! You gotta believe me!"

Ace moved his bottom close to Sam, "Don't get *cheeky* with me, mister! Something *stinks* around here, and it's not me! What's with the falling spears?"

"It was an accident, I swear!" Sam

sputtered. "I was trying to get a better look and I accidentally bumped the spear shelf. I wasn't trying to hurt you, honest!"

"Hmmm," said Ace. "I have a *haunch* you're telling the truth. Okay, you can go!"

Ace stood up and untied Sam.

"Hey! So do you think I could help you with your search?" Sam asked hopefully.

"Gee, I don't know, rookie. I've already got a semi-helpful sidekick." Ace looked around. "At least I think I do. Where's Spike?"

They found Spike in front of a dusty mirror, posing like he was a gladiator. He was wearing a tattered yellow cloth around his body like a toga.

"It seems Spike can't make up his mind if he wants to work in the detective game or show business," Ace explained to Sam coolly. "I can't believe he'd leave me for Hollywood after all those times I sang 'Itsy Bitsy Spider' to him."

Suddenly, Ace stopped. He looked at Spike's toga.

"Hey, I recognize that material! That's a piece of Sparky's cape! Well done, Spike! You found another clue!"

Spike looked at the material, puzzled. Then he pointed to several more strips of the same fabric on the floor. There was a trail of fabric leading off in one direction.

"Spike, I knew you couldn't give up pet detective work!" Ace lifted the little monkey into the air and then hugged him tightly. "You found a trail that Sparky obviously left for us to follow!"

"Ook ook-a choob," Spike blinked. *Um . . . yeah. Sure I did.*

Ace eagerly followed the yellow fabric strips out of the prop warehouse. Spike and Sam followed close behind.

"Sparky is a really clever dog, ya know? See, it took a lot of doggie smarts to think of leaving a trail of cloth strips for someone to follow . . . especially while in the clutches of some two-bit criminal!

"With my ragtag junior detectives following, I flat-footed my way across the studio lot, keeping my peepers trained for bits of Sparky's cape."

"Who's he talking to?" Sam asked Spike.

"I was talking to *you*, spare change. Now listen up, and ya might learn something, see?" Ace pointed to another building up ahead. "The trail is leading us to the costume warehouse. So peel your lips and keep your eyes buttoned."

Ace, Spike, and Sam entered the costume warehouse. It was a wondrous place, filled from floor to ceiling with every kind of costume imaginable — from cavemen furs to futuristic space suits.

"Every costume from every film made at the studio ends up here," Sam explained. "It would be fun to look at them all. But as you can clearly see, Sparky must have been carried in one door and out another."

Sam gestured to the floor. Sure enough, Sparky's torn cloth trail led across the warehouse floor and out through a door on the other side. Spike looked longingly at the costumes. He thought it was too bad they couldn't stay a while.

"Ya know, as detectives, we need a way to get around unnoticed — a disguise. But where are we going to find a disguise?" Aced mused.

He paused. Spike tugged at Ace's pant leg and pointed at the costume racks that surrounded them.

"Stop it, Spike! I'm trying to think." Spike shook his head. Then he gathered an armload of costumes and dumped them on top of Ace's head.

"Hey, Spike! Don't mess with the 'do," Ace yelled. Then he noticed the costumes and yelped with joy. He and Spike jumped into the racks of costumes and started putting on clothes. After a minute, Sam shrugged and decided to join them.

Several seconds later, Ace emerged dressed as a Spanish *conquistador,* complete with armor and a helmet.

"I am the mighty explorer Ponce Upon-A-Time, come to discover the lost city of cornflakes! But wait, who do I see walking my way?"

Out from the racks came Spike. He was dressed from head to toe like a Renaissance painter. He even wore a painter's cap and carried a brush.

"Why it's the famous Italian scientist and master artist, Leonardo da Anthropoid!" Ace grinned and saluted Spike. "Good day, Master Leo!"

Spike bowed and gave a twirl of his hand.

"And I am Little Bo-Peep, and I have lost my sheep! And I am *ever* so upset! Boo-hoo-hoo!" Sam emerged dressed in a blue dress with a white petticoat and apron. His legs were in pantaloons and he wore a blond wig done up in pigtails. In his gloved hands, he carried a shepherd's staff.

He looked really odd. Ace and Spike watched him in horror.

"What's the matter?" Sam asked.

Ace sighed and took off his helmet. "Oh, it's nothing. Just . . . way to ruin the image, Sam!"

"What do you mean?"

Ace looked very disappointed. "Well, Spike and I are obviously dressed up as *real* people from history . . . then you come along dressed as a Mother Goose character . . ." Ace was getting tears in his eyes. "It just wrecked everything!"

Sam was thunderstruck. "Hey, I'm really sorry! I didn't . . ."

"That's okay." Ace held out his hand, trying to be strong. "But you know what? I'll bet Ms. Astor would be real grateful for an update on our progress right about now."

Sam looked hopeful.

"Why don't you run along and give her the scoop?" Ace smiled. "I'm sure she'll remember you come raise time."

"That's a great idea," Sam beamed. "I'll go tell her! I'll go tell her right now!"

With that, Sam rushed out of the warehouse and toward Ms. Astor's office.

"Go! Go, my shepherdess of information!" Ace waved.

Sam was still wearing the Bo-Peep costume. Ace and Spike chuckled as he pulled up his dress and ran.

"Now that we've gotten rid of the loooooooser, maybe we can get to the bottom of this mystery." Ace winked. "And I think I've found the perfect things to help us along!"

Ace led Spike back into the costume racks. When they emerged again, they were both wearing trench coats and fedora hats — just like detectives in old movies!

"Alrighty then, Spike," Ace said in his detective voice. "It's time to get back to trailing that pooch, see?"

They followed the trail of yellow fabric pieces out of the warehouse and down a deserted alley to a row of soundstages. The trail led right up to one of the soundstage doors. Ace and Spike went inside.

They were suddenly transported to another world! Spaceships and meteors flew overhead! All sorts of strange alien beasts grazed on the planet's surface! They could see humanoids in space suits floating above the horizon!

Just as the shock was wearing off,

they heard strange voices behind them. They turned.

"Stop! Halt, alien intruders!"

Two ugly alien warriors were leaping down from the rocks above, coming to get them!

"The two outer space creeps chased us past a big crater. Then past some kind of space rhinoceros that looked like it had mops sticking out if its snout instead of horns.

"After thinking we'd ditched them in a transport tunnel, we realized it was just a scam. We'd moon-walked right into their little trap! Our backs up against the panels of a solar-train, Spike and I took a gander at the rummies that were gunning for us. They were ugly. *Real* ugly mugs!"

The aliens looked at each other.

"Who's he talking to?" asked one of the aliens.

"Who's an ugly mug?" said the other, his feelings hurt.

"Cut!" came a voice from across the soundstage. "Print! Excellent!"

The aliens grabbed Ace and Spike and dragged them over to where a large, rotund man sat in a director's chair next to a movie camera.

"Ah, you must be the one they call . . . leader," Ace said dramatically.

"We're sorry, Mr. Gutman!" one of the aliens pushed them forward. "We thought this guy was trying to steal one of the monkey actors."

"Oh, it's only a movie set!" Ace said, relieved. "*Whew!* For a second there, I thought we'd crossed over to some strange, bizarre world! You know, like stepping into the Twilight Zone . . . or driving through New Jersey."

The director turned out to be the famous Sydney Gutman, who had directed over fifty films. When he learned who Ace and Spike were, and about their mission to find Sparky, Gutman was noticeably upset.

"Sparky is missing? Good riddance, I say! Ever since those stupid 'Dog Sparky' movies have gotten so popular, I've had to make silly films that involve animals — like this one, *Planet of the Mutant Space Cows. Bah!*"

Looking at the ground bitterly, Gutman noticed Spike for the first time.

"Brillant! You saved the scene. And speaking of animals, here's a fine-looking fellow! Have you ever thought about a career in pictures, son?"

"Doop oob ook chee." Spike was obviously flattered. *Well, now that you mention it . . .*

Ace picked Spike up and carried him away. "No! No, he hasn't, and he never will! Now if you'll ex-squeeze us, we have some investigating to do!"

"Pity," said the big man. "Well, if you ever change your mind, give me a call. We'll do lunch."

"And a salami, salami, baloney to you, too! Ta-ta now. Buh-bye!"

As Ace and Spike crossed the moon-scape set, the pet detective frowned at the little monkey.

"Spike, you've got to stop encouraging these guys! You wouldn't really rather be a big Hollywood star, would you?"

Spike didn't answer. The truth was, he wasn't sure.

While the movie people were setting up their next shot, Ace and Spike took the opportunity to ask one of the stars of the film a few questions. They talked to a milk cow who had been spray-painted green and was wearing a beeping electronic helmet on her head.

Ace, of course, had the extraordinary talent of being able to talk to all sorts of animals — even green cows.

The cow said she *had* seen something strange the day before. A person wearing dark clothes had scurried through the soundstage carrying a bundle. Whatever was in that bundle seemed to be whimpering! The cow nodded at a side door, showing them where the person had exited.

Ace and Spike took the cue and headed for the door. They had to circle around a huge satellite dish and a herd of purple sheep. They stepped out the door into a narrow alley between soundstages. The door to the next soundstage was directly across.

"I'll bet dollars to dodo birds that the dognapper took Sparky in there, Spike!"

Suddenly, Ace and Spike were mobbed from all sides by a bunch of screaming people asking questions. After a moment of confusion, Ace realized that they were reporters from newspapers and TV stations.

"Mr. Ventura, is it true Sparky, the celebrity sheep dog, has been stolen?"

"Do you have any leads?"

"Do you think Sparky's been abducted by a UFO?"

"Any chance you'll bring in a fortune-teller to help you?"

"Hey, isn't that Spike the wonder monkey? Can I have your autograph?"

"Puh-lease!" Ace cried. "We have no statement at this time . . . Spike!"

Spike was preening for one of the TV cameras. Ace grabbed the little monkey by the collar and pulled him through the next door.

"It's a jungle out there . . . and in here, too!"

Inside was a terrific set that looked like a jungle in deepest South America. All around were trees and hanging vines with beautiful, exotic flowers.

"Now, that's better," Ace sighed.

But Spike wasn't so sure. He tugged at Ace's trench coat and pointed down.

They were standing knee-deep in quicksand!

Chapter 9

Deeper and deeper they sank. It wasn't long before Ace was up to his waist in the thick mud. He pulled Spike out and set the spunky little monkey up on his shoulders.

Ace would have insisted Spike jump for it. But the quicksand pool was too wide, and they'd walked right into the middle of it. Things looked pretty dim.

"Spike, my fuzzy buddy, if we don't think of something fast, we're going to end up in that big pet palace in the sky!"

Looking up, Spike saw something that brought a smile to his furry face. He excitedly jumped up and down on Ace's shoulders.

"Hey, hey, Spike! What are you trying to do, sink me faster?"

Spike grabbed Ace's chin and forced his gaze upward. The pet detective saw what Spike was pointing at.

"Way to go, my eagle-eyed primate protégé! It's a boa constrictor, from the family *Boidae,* related to the python and usually found in the jungles of Central and South America."

Up in the tree overhead was indeed a long, long, LOOOOONG boa, quietly taking a nap. The snake was obviously one of the stars of the jungle movie being filmed there.

Ace hissed up at the snake in the tree. After a moment, the snake hissed back. Ace hissed again and the big boa nodded his head.

Swiftly, the boa wrapped his tail around the branch he was sitting on. Then he stretched down to where Ace and Spike were stuck. When the snake was close enough, they grabbed hold of its neck. The snake was so strong, it easily lifted them out of the muddy trap and gently set them on dry ground. They were saved!

"A thousand thanks, my serpentine savior!" Ace cheered. "Whoa! Do not go in there!"

Ace and Spike hugged the boa. The boa hugged back — a little too tightly.

"*Urk!* Okay! Enough with the hugging!" Ace gasped, short of breath.

They said good-bye to the snake and made their way through the dense jungle setting. Before long, they came to a clearing where a big, muscular man wearing nothing but a tiger-skin loincloth was sitting in a lounge chair, reading a newspaper.

"Hey, I know you!" Ace grinned. "You're Johnny Weisenheimer, star of all those 'Jungle Jim' movies!"

The man looked up from reading his newspaper and pouted. "That's right, but no autographs today! It's lunch break and I'm trying to read the gossip column."

Ace nudged Spike and pointed to the newspaper Johnny was reading. On the cover was a big picture of Sparky, the celebrity sheepdog. The headline read DOG GONE SPARKY! Underneath was a picture of Spike, running away from reporters, with the caption NEW SUPERSTAR MONKEY DISCOVERED!

"Boy, those press guys sure work fast!" Ace blinked.

While Spike wandered around, Ace asked Johnny if he knew anything about Sparky's disappearance. At the mention of Sparky's name, Johnny curtly folded up his newspaper and threw it on the ground. He stood up to his full height — almost seven feet tall. He stretched and flexed his muscles.

"The only thing I know about Sparky is that I'm glad he's gone!" Johnny sniffed. "That dog is *so* unprofessional!" Johnny put his hands on his hips, "Why, do you know he actually bit me once at a party? He bit me!" Johnny looked around to make sure no one else was listening.

"How was I supposed to know I was standing on his cape?"

Ace asked Johnny if he'd noticed anything unusual the day before. Johnny said he had. A person had run through the jungle carrying a lumpy bundle and disappeared through the loading-dock doors on the north side of the soundstage.

"Whoever it was, they were dressed like they had something to hide. Simply atrocious attire!" Johnny frowned, then he looked over at Spike. "Say, is that the great new monkey actor everyone's raving about?"

Ace's smile was icy. "No . . . no, he's not."

"Then tell him to get his paws out of my bagel basket!" Johnny said, stalking off in a huff to his dressing room.

Ace scooped up his always-hungry monkey, and they went to investigate the loading dock.

The dock looked like a loading area

you'd find at almost every warehouse. It was a place where big objects could be loaded on or off big trucks. Across the parking lot from the dock was an open gate. The gate led to a side street and then to a big boulevard. If the dognapper had taken Sparky out this way, he or she could be anywhere by now.

"*Chee oop a-chee choo!*" Spike said in a disappointed tone. *The trail's gone cold!*

"Never fear, Spike! For when the going gets tough, Ace Ventura gets rough! And if you can't stand the heat, don't live in a glass house. A stitch in time saves nine!"

Spike blinked at Ace. *Now* what was Ace talking about?

"What I'm trying to say, Mighty Joe Tiny, is that I've an idea how to solve this mystery." Ace grinned. "But I'm going to have to make a few phone calls first!"

Spike handed Ace his own personal cell phone.

Chapter 10

"It was a warm and muggy night — mainly because we were all drinking warm mugs of cocoa, with tiny marshmallows floating at the top.

"I had gathered all the suspects to meet me in an old, creepy house on the set of a horror movie that was being filmed on the studio lot. It was dark and quiet . . . the perfect place to solve a crime. I turned to the assembled suspects and declared . . . *one of you in this room is a dognapper.*"

Everyone gasped.

"First we have Sydney Gutman, the hefty veteran director who hates Sparky because the dog's movies are more popular than his!

"Then we have Sam Shovel, the shifty-eyed studio detective who might have stolen Sparky only to help find him — and get a big raise.

"Of course, we can't forget the brother

and sister team of Philip and Liz Astor, who may be working together to replace Sparky with Philip's client, Duke.

"Last, but not least, Johnny Weisenheimer, the egotistical actor whom Sparky bit.

"And to round out our little shindig, I've also invited Duke the dog, the snake who saved our lives, and three of the purple space-sheep, just for color."

"This is a waste of time!" growled Philip Astor. The other suspects started to grumble, too.

"Oh ree-hee-heally?" Ace frowned. "In all good mystery stories, there's always a gathering like this! And the villain is *always* discovered during these get-togethers."

"Ventura, you idiot!" barked Sydney Gutman. "Somebody almost always ends up *dead* at one of these gatherings, too!"

"Ooh, yeah," Ace said, caught off guard. "I forgot about *that*!"

The room grew silent. Then, suddenly . . .

The lights went out!

"Not that again!" Ace cried.

Someone started screaming — a high, shrill scream. "*Eeeeeeeeeeeeeeeek!*"

There were sounds of a tussle that lasted several seconds. Finally, when the lights came back on . . . nothing had changed.

They all looked around. Johnny Weisenheimer was still screaming at the top of his lungs. After a moment, the others got Johnny to calm down.

"I told you this was a ridiculous waste of time!" Philip Astor sneered.

"Not at all, Monsieur Nosebent." Ace walked proudly over to a window. "For I have the dognapper right where I want him!"

Ace opened the window and reached through it. When he pulled back, he was clutching the collar of the ratlike Hollywood agent, Frankie Fester. Everyone stared in surprise.

"Let me go," Frankie squealed. "You can't prove a thing!"

"Why would Frankie dognap his own client?" Ms. Astor was puzzled.

"I'm sooooo glad you asked," Ace took a deep breath. "Frankie dognapped Sparky so he could get one of the most valuable things in Hollywood — free publicity."

Ace held up the newspaper with Sparky's picture on the front. "Frankie knew that if Sparky was lost and then found, his next movie would make a fortune! That's why he hired me and Spike. Bringing the world's most famous pet detective on the case was sure to get attention. To make sure we stayed interested, he warned us off the case. Then he tried to kidnap Duke to prevent him from taking Sparky's spot."

"*Hmmm.* Free publicity. Why didn't I think of that?" Ms. Astor pondered.

"Spike and I followed Sparky's trail through the studio and it turned out to be a wild-goose chase," Ace continued. "So I asked myself which one of you suspects had the most to gain.

"Acting on a hunch, I went to Frankie's office. I knew Frankie would come snooping around here once he heard I was gathering all the suspects. So I waited for him to leave his office and then went inside.

"Guess what I found?" Ace walked over to a door and opened it. Out bounded Sparky, the celebrity sheepdog.

Everyone looked at Frankie. "But-But-But . . ." he stuttered.

"But wait!" Ace grinned. "I think you'll want to see what's behind door number two!"

Ace opened the next door, and reporters rushed in, taking pictures and asking questions.

"Congratulations, Frankie, you've got all the free publicity you could ever hope for! But that's not all . . . what's behind door number three?"

Ace opened yet another door. Behind it were two policemen.

"You get something extra — a free trip to the Hollywood jail!"

The policemen grabbed Frankie and led him out. The reporters mobbed the celebrities and took them aside. Philip Astor was asking Sparky if he needed a new agent.

Ace did his victory dance with his partner. "Can ya feel it, Spike? Yes! Yes! Yes!"

When Ace had finished dancing, Ms. Astor approached him.

"Well, Mr. Ventura, I seem to have misjudged you," she said. "The studio is in your debt. How can we ever repay you?"

"Easy," Ace smiled. "Here's my bill!"

He unrolled a piece of paper that was as least twice as long as the contract Hank Henderson had offered Spike earlier.

Ms. Astor took the bill with a smirk.

"Let's talk real money, Ace. I'd like to make a film about your exploits. What do you say?"

Ace was flattered, but he had to decline. "Sorry, Ms. Astor. A movie about Ace Ventura, Pet Detective? Who'd pay to see that? That's a terrible idea! Besides, I prefer to keep my exploits anonymous."

Ms. Astor shrugged, then she looked down at Spike.

"What about you, Spike? All the directors in town want to work with you. Think of how glamorous a career in the movies would be. I could sign you up right now!"

"Spike could never leave a rewarding life of pet detecting for a life of starlets, limos, and fancy restaurants, would you Spike?" Ace asked.

Spike looked from Ace to Ms. Astor.

"Er . . . b-because it would mean trading a loyal partnership for hot-tub parties." Ace was worried now.

Spike looked from Ms. Astor to Ace.

Then he slowly started walking toward Ms. Astor, looking longingly at the contract.

"Alrighty, then, Spike!" Ace was frantic. "I'll give you *half* the detective fees, if you'll just stay with me!"

After thinking a moment . . . Spike agreed to stay with Ace! (He had never really intended to leave, he just wanted something extra out of the deal.) Now it was the little monkey's chance to do some dancing. *Yes! Yes! Yes! That's a lot of dough, sweetheart!*

Ace joined Spike and they danced out of the movie studio and into a waiting limousine.

In fact, they danced *inside* the limo, all the way back to the airport.

And so, another animal is saved, another Ace case solved.

Fun Animal Facts From the Ace Case Files

Who's your main squeeze? As the name implies, boa constrictors (like the one in this story) kill their prey by squeezing, or constricting them until the animal suffocates. Most boas only eat small mammals, but some are so big and muscular, they can capture and swallow pigs and goats. How's that for getting your goat?

Wake up! You may think your dad is lazy on Sunday afternoons, but he's no match for the sloth, the armadillo, or the opossum. Did you know that these animals sleep or snooze four-fifths of their lives? No wonder they've never had a good basketball team!

Light as a bird? Think again! The male African ostrich is the largest bird in the world. Some have grown to the height of nine feet and the weight of 345 pounds!

Not only that, they are the fastest land birds, able to reach speeds up to forty miles per hour. Some people mistake them for speedsters and use them to race!

A home is a home is a bat cave! Different species of bats have different tastes in where they want to live. Some hang out in trees, some in rock crevices, some in caves. Other places they like to call home are mines, tunnels, attics, old buildings, and bridges. Ace doesn't care where they live, as long as it's not with him. *Eeeeeeew!*

Productive? You don't know the half of it! Everyone knows that dairy cows produce a lot of milk, but do you know about the *other* things they bring forth? They have been known to produce up to 125 pounds of saliva a day, as well as 200 pounds of flatus (that's passed gas, like burps and you-know-what!) Bet they don't get invited to many parties!

Well, alrighty then!